POLAR BOND

EMERALD CITY SHIFTERS — BOOK TWO

ARIA CHASE

DEMIMONDE PRESS

Cover Design © 2017 Rebecca Pau / The Final Wrap

Polar Bond / Aria Chase. -- 1st ed.

An Ordinary Girl

While visiting Seattle for her best friend's wedding, curvy Grace DiPlaski is immediately attracted to the best man. When he reciprocates her feelings, lavishes her with expensive gifts, and introduces her to pleasure unlike anything she's ever known, Grace feels herself falling for him — and falling fast. So why does she get the feeling that he's too good to be true?

An Extraordinary Attraction

Kingston Meade knew Grace was his mate the moment he laid eyes on her. He's determined to claim her and show her what passion truly means — but only on his terms. He knows he can offer her *almost* everything a woman wants, but the one thing he can't promise is total honesty. Their magnetic pull to one another is undeniable, but Kingston can't call it love — not with such a massive secret hanging between them.

A Dangerous World

But when panther shifter Ashley views Grace as a threat, Grace's previously ordinary life is turned upside down. Ashley is determined to get her claws into Kingston, and she's willing to slash Grace out of his life to do it. When Kingston realizes he may lose her forever, will he brave enough to share his secret and find a way to save his curvy human queen?

STAY IN TOUCH

Sign up for Aria's newsletter to keep up with new paranormal romance and urban fantasy releases, win bookish giveaways, receive opportunities for advance review copies, and more.

Love is our true destiny.
We do not find the meaning of life by ourselves alone—
we find it with another.

— THOMAS MERTON

1

As she seated herself at the table, the first thing Grace noticed was the bewildering array of silverware choices. It was far different from her typical life in Calgary, where each meal came with a single fork, knife, and spoon. She knew Breanna had grown up in this world, so her friend seemed completely at ease with the silverware when she sneaked a peek at the bride and groom farther down the table.

Unlike the bride-to-be, Grace had grown up with humbler roots, more middle-class comfortable than old money wealthy. If it hadn't been for Breanna's parents being such judgmental jerks, she supposed she never would have met her best friend. They had considered it a punishment to send their daughter to state university—whereas Grace had considered it a privilege to attend UCLA, especially on scholarship—but their prejudices had created the perfect situation for the two girls who started as roommates to become best friends.

Which was what brought her to this table now, staring at the silverware. A glance to her right revealed an older woman selecting a fork from the outside for the salad, so she did the same.

A second later, all thoughts of silverware or anything else left her mind as the empty seat beside hers was filled. She glanced up, way up, to see who the late arrival was. She knew he had to be the best man, Kingston Meade, but they hadn't met yet. According to Rafe, he was in the middle of a merger that took a lot of time and attention.

"Sorry I'm late, old buddy, but it took forever to get Yamato to stop yammering," he said to the groom.

The new arrival was handsome. Handsome didn't even begin to cover it really. He had fine, sculpted cheekbones, pale gray eyes, and platinum-blonde hair styled in careless waves around his face. With broad shoulders that filled out his gray evening jacket in a mouthwatering fashion, she couldn't help imagining what she would find under that outfit, were her hands at liberty to discover for themselves. That thought, entirely inappropriate, caused her panties to grow damp.

Suddenly, the best man stiffened, his nostrils flaring as his head turned toward her. He didn't speak for a moment, his pale gray eyes somehow darkening slightly, looking more intense. There was a hint of watchfulness about him, almost like a predator sensing prey. No, that didn't seem quite right either. It was an indefinable quality, something with which she was unfamiliar, but for some reason, increased her arousal and made her nipples crinkle against the cream-colored sweater dress. She was thankful for the thick cable pattern that hid her reaction.

A moment later, he blinked, and the intensity was gone. He gave her a charming smile and held out a hand. "I don't think we've met. You must be Grace?"

She nodded, taking his hand and feeling clumsy as she did so. "Yes, I'm Grace DiPlaski. You must be Kingston?"

Instead of just shaking her hand, he did something unexpected. He turned it over and brought it to his mouth, pressing his lips lightly to her knuckles before returning her hand to her. "Yes. I'll admit I've been dreading the amount of time this wedding would require, and it's not even my own, but it's suddenly seeming a lot more fun. It's my understanding we get to spend a lot of time together."

She resisted the urge to giggle like an infatuated teenager, because she wasn't a teenager. The infatuated part wasn't far off the mark, she had to concede. Somehow, she sounded confident and airy when she replied, "I think it's one of the perks of the jobs."

"I'm sure your boyfriend or husband will miss your time though." It was a statement, not a question, but he was watching her closely as he sipped the white wine accompanying the first course at the rehearsal dinner.

She shook her head, feeling not even a twinge of regret that she had broken up with her longtime boyfriend just weeks ago. Before this minute, she had wished they had managed to make it past the wedding, so she'd have a plus-one for the event, not because she missed anything about her boring, stuffy ex-boyfriend. Now, she was relieved not to have a plus-one, though common sense dictated Kingston was only being polite, or perhaps indulging in a bit of light-hearted flirtation that would probably go nowhere.

Grace was pretty, and she knew it. With thick brown hair that curled riotously around her head without careful maintenance, honey-bronzed skin that was her natural complexion without foundation, and brown eyes, she got her fair share of second (and third) looks.

She was also curvy. Excessively curvy, by many standards. It didn't bother her that her clothes came from the plus-size department, because she loved her hourglass figure. A lot of guys appreciated it too, but in her experience, not the type like Kingston Meade.

He was a powerful businessman, the CEO of his company according to Rafe, and far more likely to date the typical standard of beauty, like a supermodel or an actress. She would have been a superstar during the Renaissance, but she was very much outside the conventional norms of beauty for today.

Of course, she might be wrong, she conceded, as she glanced at him from the side of her eye and caught his gaze resting blatantly on the swell of her curvy breasts, pressing against the cashmere fabric. The dress had been an expensive indulgence, one that had taken a good part of her monthly salary as a records clerk at Calgary Registry Services, but she couldn't regret having splurged on it with the way his eyes couldn't seem to tear away from her curves. It was the exact reaction she had been looking for when she had tried on the dress and plunked down her credit card with a small gulp.

"No, I don't have a boyfriend to worry about monopolizing my time. I assume your wife or girlfriend must be feeling somewhat resentful your responsibilities to the wedding, coupled with your merger?"

He took a moment to finish chewing the bite of Caesar salad, clearly relishing the anchovy melting in his mouth. "I don't have a wife or girlfriend."

"Boyfriend, perhaps?" she asked, carefully probing for information.

He shook his head. "Not one of those either, and I'm not in the market. To be honest, finding a mate was last thing on my mind...until recently."

Mate seemed like an odd word, but she supposed it fit. It always made her think of animals, like wolves or bears, mating for life. In some ways, it was a deeper-sounding commitment than marriage, which could end on a whim. Deciding she rather liked the term, she asked, "What changed your mind?"

"Love is in the air," he said with a hint of sarcasm alleviated by his playful wink. His gaze darted to Rafe and Breanna, who were busy feeding each other bites off their plates, though they had the same meals, and seemed oblivious to the people around them.

"No kidding. They're almost sickening, aren't they?" She didn't really mean that, of course. In fact, Grace was envious of their happiness. She certainly didn't begrudge Breanna having found someone she wanted to marry and spend her life with, but it underscored Grace's own loneliness.

Peter had been a fine substitute for a real relationship, and at times, he had been preferable to being alone, but she'd always known she wouldn't end up with him. There wasn't enough of a spark between them, and he was also kind of an asshole.

He had hidden that in the beginning, but it became more obvious as time progressed. She was happier alone now than she had been with him, but that didn't mean she wanted to embrace a life of solitude, and certainly not celibacy. "It must be nice," she said with a soft sigh.

"And kind of scary, to want someone so much, to need that person to the extent that your own happiness is all twined up with theirs. If something happens to them, you know you'll be miserable for the rest of your life. Sounds kind of frightening to want someone that much."

She arched a brow. "When you put it like that, I guess

there is a strong component of fear, but that doesn't make me want it any less."

"Me either," he said, his voice rich with a hint of envy of his own.

The conversation changed to more lighthearted topics, and they became better acquainted as the meal progressed. By the time strawberry shortcake dishes, left in various states of completion, were whisked from the table, she was pleasantly relaxed, both from the food and his company.

There was a strong hint of awareness though, so she couldn't completely relax. It was as though they were attuned to each other, and her body buzzed just being near him. She couldn't imagine what it would feel like to have him actually touch her, but she sure wanted to know.

A few moments later, the band started playing a waltz, and he held out his hand. "Shall we?"

"Don't be silly," said a sharp voice from behind them. "It's kind of you to invite her to dance, Kingston, but I imagine a big girl like her would feel awkward on the dance floor."

Grace flinched at the words, uttered from such a bitchy mouth. Turning her head, she identified the source as a tall, slinky woman, who probably wore a negative dress size. There was something feline about her, perhaps in the way she moved, or maybe it was the way she purred Kingston's name. She seemed like a cat about to pounce on a disabled mouse.

Grace had never even spoken to the woman, and she had no idea who she was, but she wasn't a mouse. Whatever the reason for the woman's rude comment, she wasn't going to let it stand. Without speaking to the other woman, she turned her attention back to Kingston and extended her hand. "I'd love to." She couldn't deny a surge of satisfaction at the other woman's disgruntled expression when they walked past her, still hand-in-hand, and moved to the dance floor.

Held securely in his arms, closer than propriety dictated, she wasn't going to complain.

"I apologize for Ashley. She can be quite caustic at times. She's an old family friend, so I'm kind of stuck with her."

She followed his lead easily, thankful her mother had insisted on four years of ballroom dancing when Grace would have preferred jazz and tap. She was confident in her moves, easily matching his rhythm, as her body curled into his. Her soft curves nestled against the firm planes of his body, and her nipples hardened further. New wetness flooded her sodden panties as they pressed together, moving through the waltz with ease. "That's okay. Unless you raised her, I doubt you're to blame for her lack of manners."

He shuddered. "That would be a thankless task. I sort of pity her parents, but they overindulged her. She was an only child."

"So is Breanna, but her parents certainly didn't overindulge her."

Kingston nodded, his expression bordering on sad. "She told me a little bit about growing up in the Dawson household. Sounds like it was rough."

"Yes, it does." When she had first met Breanna, she had envied the other woman's wealth and seeming ease of acquiring anything she needed in life.

It hadn't taken long to get better acquainted with her shy roommate and realize that while her parents had everything money could buy, they were stingy with doling it out to their daughter unless she lived up to their unreasonable expectations. They were even more miserly with love and affection. Once or twice, Grace had tried to gently suggest that

Breanna not worry so much about what her parents thought, but it had seemed to upset her roommate, so she'd avoided the subject.

Things had certainly changed since Breanna met Rafe. Her best friend was now a confident woman, held firmly in her soon-to-be husband's embrace.

Kingston was holding her just as firmly, she realized, and each deep breath she took pressed her breasts against his chest and further sensitized her nipples. She had the mad urge to tear open his dress shirt, rip off his tie, and press her sweater-covered breasts against his bare chest. Thankfully, it was a passing fancy, and she had it under control before she could even so much as reach for the first button on his pearl-gray shirt.

When the music ended, she started to step back, but his arms tightened again, pulling her even closer. It was an unsubtle hint that he wasn't done with her, but that was fine, because she wasn't done with him either.

It had been a long time, if ever, that she had spent the night dancing in her lover's arms. Kingston wasn't her lover, but she didn't think she was completely crazy to entertain the idea that he would be at some point. Her best friend's wedding was the perfect opportunity to indulge in a harmless fling, though Grace wasn't really the fling type.

She'd never been able to sleep with someone she had just met, even if there was an intense attraction. Admittedly, she'd never been so attracted to someone so instantly before in her life. It went completely against her nature, but she couldn't guarantee she would turn him down if he bent her over the dessert table right now and feasted on her feminine essence. The thought made her whimper lightly, and her thigh muscles tightened involuntarily in reaction to the dart of arousal shooting through her core.

Kingston growled softly, an honest-to-goodness growl that was more animalistic than human. It was a sexy sound, albeit strange. She looked up at him, noticing again how tall he was compared to her. She was already on the short side, but he seemed like he had to be extremely tall, at least 6'4".

"Are you all right?" It was an inane question, and it wasn't what she really wanted to ask. Somehow, she bit back the urge to ask him if he wanted to slip away to the coat closet. Since it was April, there would probably still be some coats in there to hide their activities. Reminding herself she wasn't the exhibitionist type, any more than she was the type to hop into bed with a stranger, she bit back the urge.

"No," he said in a half-growl. That intense look was back again, the one that made her feel hunted, but not fearful of being caught. The idea of him chasing her down and taking her sent a thrill of dark pleasure through her rather than one of fear. "Is there something I can do to help?"

His body thrummed with energy, and he seemed to be on the verge of saying something deliciously wicked, but a cool splash down her back and side made her gasp and distracted her. Grace pulled away from him to find the source of discomfort, shocked to see red wine bleeding through the soft cashmere cream dress.

Stricken, she looked up to meet the cold eyes of Ashley, holding an empty wine glass. Her smirk of satisfaction fooled no one when she said, "Oh dear, how clumsy of me. Well, you must run along and clean up." Without glancing at Grace again, she turned to Kingston, neatly sliding her body into the space between them. She wrapped her arms around his neck and pressed her slender body to his. "It looks like you need a dance partner."

Grace had to resist the urge to grab a handful of the strange white hair of the woman who had just doused her very expensive dress with a very expensive Burgundy wine. From a distance, she had thought Ashley was another platinum-blonde, but up close, she could see her hair was actually white. It was strangely beautiful, and the woman herself was beautiful everywhere except her attitude.

With a small sigh of surrender, knowing she needed to get the dress off and tend to the stains as quickly as possible if she had any hope of saving the expensive garment, she turned away from them and rushed from the ballroom of the hotel hosting the reception dinner. The nearest ladies' room was right across the hall, and she ducked inside.

It wasn't ideal, but she would have to dab at the dress she wore before running up to her room. She would send it immediately down to be laundered, but she wasn't hopeful that the hotel could save it either. She had just gotten a handful of wet paper towels when the door opened, and her best friend slipped inside.

Breanna wore an expression of concern, and she crossed the bathroom quickly on high heels that tapped with every move. Her straight posture and confident pose was a stark contrast to the shy and timid woman she'd been before Rafe. "What happened?"

Grace shrugged. "To be honest, I'm not sure. I mean, I know what happened, but I don't know why." She quickly recounted for Breanna the story of how her dress became stained, along with the catty remark Ashley had made to her earlier before she started dancing with Kingston.

"She's jealous," said Breanna firmly. There wasn't a hint of doubt in her voice.

Grace laughed softly as she dabbed at the wine spots. Little specks of paper towel stuck to the white fabric, and she knew she was fighting a losing battle. "What? Why would she be jealous of me? Have you seen her? I mean she's a little strange-looking, with her pale skin and that white hair, but she's beautiful."

"She's leucistic. Kind of like a form of albinism," said Breanna.

Grace nodded. "I didn't know the term, but I thought it might be something like that. I wasn't sure though, since she doesn't have pink eyes like most albino animals."

"They should be bright green instead of that pale blue, because the girl is green with envy. It's no secret she wants Kingston, and she's always bugging him. There's the answer for you. She was jealous of the time he's spending with you. Clearly, she realizes he wants you, and she wants to make sure that doesn't happen."

Grace wanted to believe her friend, but she was assailed by an unexpected dart of self-doubt. It was the same one that had come to her earlier, reminding her men like him dated supermodels, not super-curvy girls. "I still don't think she has anything to worry about."

Breanna cocked her head slightly, sending caramel-brown waves fluttering down her shoulder. "Really? You're really going to stand there and pretend like we didn't need to have the fire department on standby with you two heating up the floor like that?"

Her cheeks flamed. "You're one to talk. You and Rafe were practically humping on the floor."

Breanna laughed, clearly not going to deny it. "The difference is, we're already mated—I mean engaged, and about to be married, so there's no reason to deny our attraction. The question is, my dear, why are you denying his for you and yours for him?"

"I'm not denying I'm attracted to him, but I just find it hard to believe I might be his type. I am a sexy piece, but I have a feeling guys like him go for girls like Ashley, not me."

Breanna snorted. "If that were the case, he could've gone for her night after night. The chick is not subtle. Don't worry about her, because he's clearly not interested in Ashley Toth. He's interested in Grace DiPlaski." With a firm nod, she glanced at the doorway. "I have to get back to the party. Are you all right?"

Grace nodded. "I will be. I'm going to slip up to my room and try to send this down to the laundry to see if they can salvage it." Thinking of the amount on her credit card, waiting to be paid off, she could have cried at the waste. Either that, or plucked every white hair out of Ashley's head.

"If you won't feel offended though, I'll probably just stay in for the rest of the night. I don't have another fancy outfit with me, aside from my dress for the wedding and what I'm wearing to the bachelorette party tomorrow night, and I'm just kind of drained after the whole Ashley Toth experience."

Breanna gave her a quick hug, careful to avoid the side splashed with red wine so as not to stain her own pale gold dress. "Of course, Grace. Just unwind and forget all about Ashley, but don't discount Kingston. I don't know him as well as I know Rafe, of course, but I think I know him well enough to tell when he's attracted to someone. He wants you."

"Well, let's see if he takes me." She winked at her friend as Breanna departed before spending another five futile minutes trying to wipe away the stains. With a sigh, she conceded defeat and tossed the paper towels into the trash can. After washing her hands and drying them with another round of paper towels, she walked to the door. When she opened it, her heart leapt in her chest, and she pressed a hand to it as though to hold it in. "You startled me."

Kingston leaned against the doorway, a white robe held

out to her. "Sorry. I was just waiting for you to come out. I had the hotel concierge secure this for you. I thought you might want to put it on and get out of that wet dress." His eyes moved to her breasts, where the splotch of wine had spread across her left side, making her bra and beaded nipple visible on that side.

"Thank you." She reached for the robe and started to slide it on over the dress, moved by his thoughtfulness almost as much as the lust she saw shining in his eyes. Breanna was right. He wanted her, and she wanted him.

It was an untenable position, simply because she wasn't certain about indulging in a temporary relationship. What else could it be, with him living in Seattle and her in Calgary? She'd be the first to admit her job as a records clerk wasn't exactly career material, and she wouldn't be opposed to relocating to Seattle for the right man, but she still didn't think the relationship would go anywhere besides the bedroom.

"Take off the dress first." That growl was back in his voice, and his eyes had darkened again.

She shivered under the gaze, surprised to find her hands moving to the hem of her dress. She wasn't really going to take off the garment standing in the open doorway of the ladies' bathroom, was she? She hesitated with her fingers at the hemline, staring at him uncertainly.

"Please, take it off. I want to see you."

Forgetting all about anyone who might come by, and already knowing she had the ladies' room to herself, at least for the moment, Grace obeyed his commands. She wasn't really the submissive type, but he was just so commanding, and that intense edge surrounding him made her want to do whatever he said. She pulled off the soggy dress and extended it to him to trade for the robe he had taken back.

He held it carefully as he handed her the robe, his gaze not wavering from her body as she slipped on the terrycloth. She hadn't tied the tie yet when he spoke again.

"Take off your bra."

She stared at him, a new wave of uncertainty sweeping over her. Grace nibbled on her full lower lip as she hesitantly reached for the front clasp of the bra. It was one of her favorites, also a new purchase.

The creamy satin was light enough to be unnoticeable under the cream-colored dress, and it provided adequate support for her larger-than-average breasts, while still making her feel ultra-feminine with the pearl and bow accent, coupled with a flirty front clasp. Her hands shook slightly, with anticipation instead of anxiety, as she opened her bra, leaving the straps on her shoulders. Her breasts sprang free, and his deep inhale was gratifying to hear.

A millisecond later, the unwelcome sound of heels tapping on the marble floor penetrated through the haze of passion trying to overtake her. Quickly, she pulled the robe closed and tied the sash, completely covered by the time their unwanted visitor came into sight.

She wasn't surprised to see Ashley standing behind Kingston, a possessive hand dropping onto his bicep. "I wondered where you had disappeared to, darling?"

Kingston shrugged her off, but the hand came back immediately. "What are you doing here, Ashley? Have you come to apologize?"

Ashley giggled, an annoyingly high-pitched sounds. "Why should I apologize when she's the clumsy one who hit my arm?"

How the story had changed already. As Kingston called her on that, Grace took advantage of the moment to slip away quietly. She was in no mood to face down the other woman, and she wasn't certain she would get through it without ripping out a few hairs and perhaps marring that pretty face. Grace wasn't a scrapper by nature, but she could hold her own if she had to. She didn't want to end up with a black eye or something equally unfortunate for her friend's wedding pictures though.

Most of all, she escaped from Kingston and her own reaction. She wanted him with intensity that overrode common sense and her normal behavior. She had to think long and hard about if she could really handle a short-term affair. By the time she got to the point where she committed her body, her mind was already committed. It had been that way for her previous relationships, and though each had fizzled out or blown up spectacularly, depending on the circumstances, she had known her partners well at least in the beginning.

Maybe what she needed was something completely different. Maybe that's where she had gone wrong. Instead of trying to get to know her partners and connect with them beyond the physical level, maybe she should just surrender to her own biological imperative and jump on Kingston the next time the opportunity arose. She still hadn't decided on that as she fished the key card from her tiny evening purse and entered the room.

As she stepped inside, she let out a small groan of realization. Her dress was still in Kingston's hand, assuming Ashley hadn't torn it from him and ripped it into pieces in a snit. She should do something about retrieving it, but she was just too frazzled to face going back downstairs tonight. She didn't want to run into Ashley, and she still wasn't confident she could withstand Kingston's charms if she sought him out, even for something as innocuous as retrieving her dress.

Instead, she used her cell phone and texted Breanna to ask her to fetch the dress after the party was over. A hot shower restored some of her equanimity, along with removing the sticky wine feeling, and she slid between the sheets naked shortly thereafter. She had never enjoyed wearing nightgowns or pajamas, and now as an adult, she reveled in sleeping nude.

Despite her uncertainty and her exhaustion from the evening, she couldn't seem to turn off her mind as it insisted on spinning fantasies of Kingston in the bed with her, equally nude, their bodies pressed together. She could feel his hands on her in her imagination, and he would be silky smooth to the touch too, except where she ran into crisp chest hair, or perhaps the hair shielding his tender sac.

She could easily imagine wrapping her hands around his shaft, certain he would be large and well-endowed just judging by how big he was everywhere else. Her mouth watered at the thought of tasting him, and she whimpered as she pictured his head between her legs.

Her hand was a poor substitute for the imaginary tongue magic her phantom lover worked as she fantasized while stroking herself to climax. As she hovered on the edge of orgasm, Grace vowed she would shove aside her own reservations and seize the moment if there was another opportunity with Kingston. She hoped she hadn't made a mistake by walking away earlier, and that she wasn't headed toward an even bigger mistake by planning to jump in without looking.

With soul-shaking certainty, she knew she would be Kingston's lover before the wedding was over. The question remaining was: for how long?

2

L ate the next afternoon, there was a knock on her hotel door. Grace had just gotten back from a morning of activities with Breanna and a couple of other women she had met at the school where she taught music. They were due to go out for the bachelorette party in a few hours, and she had planned to take a nap. Her slumber last night had been restless, haunted with erotic dreams of Kingston, so she could use an uninterrupted stretch of sleep. When she opened the door, uncertain who to expect, it was a surprise to see one of the uniformed bell staff holding a large box. "What's this?"

The young man shrugged. "I don't know, but if you're Grace DiPlaski, it's for you."

At her nod, he held out the box, and she took it. Before she had a chance to look in her purse for tip money, the young man had saluted her with a cheerful wave and was already on his way down the hall. Feeling mildly guilty for not tipping, she bumped the door closed with her hip and carried the box to the bed.

Who would be sending her something? It couldn't be

wedding-related, because she already had the maid-of-honor dress she had brought with her from Calgary, tailored and fitted to her curves to perfection. She gasped after she pulled open the gold bow and removed the black lid to see a white sweater dress lying on a pool of pale pink tissue paper. There was a cream-colored card atop, and she lifted it to read the handwritten note inside.

Dear Grace,

The laundry staff tells me your old dress is beyond saving, and this was the closest one I could find on short notice. I hope it will be an acceptable substitute.

Kingston

Her eyes widened at the idea of him buying her a dress to replace the other when it had been stained through no fault of his. Her second thought was acceptable?

She pulled out the designer-label dress, noting how soft the cashmere was. The dress Ashley had ruined was by no means cheap, but it had been a knockoff bought at a outlet factory deal, and certainly not an original designer label.

This was soft as silk, and though it didn't have the cable pattern she had adored on the other, it had a beautiful cowl neck and a banded hemline that would be flattering and show her hourglass figure. Frowning, she read the designer's name and immediately dropped the dress. It was too expensive. Far too expensive. She couldn't accept it.

Could she?

With a soft sigh of envy, she traced her fingers over the cashmere again, wanting just once to feel something so soft and silky against her skin. There was no harm in trying it on, right? As long as she left on the tags and didn't spill anything on it, he could still return the dress when she took it back to him.

Common sense dictated this was a bad idea, and it was

leading her down a dangerous path, but she shut that bitch up quickly by stripping off her skinny jeans and tunic, tossing them haphazardly on the bed before slithering into the dress.

Slither was the right word. Or floated. Glided. Whatever the descriptor, putting it on was almost as beautiful an experience as the dress itself. The outfit slid over her head and down her curves, settling into the perfect position as though made especially for her. Of course it was the clever cut of the dress, coupled with the luxuriously soft cashmere material, that gave that impression, but she still liked the idea that the designer had just her in mind when he created this beautiful piece.

She walked to the full-length mirror on the sliding door closet, admiring the picture she presented. Unlike the creamy beige from yesterday, this dress was snowy white, a color she had thought she couldn't pull off before. It seemed it would be too stark a contrast against her skin, but instead of making her look sallow, it highlighted her eyes and gave new depth of color to her dark-brown curls.

The cowl neck could be worn bunched in front or asymmetrically draped over her shoulder, and she experimented with both ways before deciding she liked it over the shoulder better. It was a versatile piece, and she couldn't wait to try it with a black belt and knee-high boots she had at home in Calgary.

No, she couldn't do that. That would mean she would be keeping the dress. It was an extravagance from someone she barely knew, and she couldn't in good conscience accept it. Right? Even the mental question was weaker than it had been before. She had her arms around her body, enjoying the soft embrace of the dress, and looked at herself again.

She looked amazing, and it wasn't like Kingston had any

other use for the dress. It was far too much for her to accept, at least as an acquaintance, but if her instincts were correct, they would be more than acquaintances before the weekend was over. It was a dress she could accept from a lover, no matter how brief the relationship lasted.

Feeling like she was justifying it to herself, a twinge of guilt accompanied the decision to keep the garment, but she tried to shrug it off. Kingston clearly knew his budget, and he wouldn't have exceeded it for a stranger, even one to whom he was attracted, or at least it wasn't likely that he would have, so there was no harm in keeping the dress. She removed the tags with a quick tug. *No turning back now.*

It wasn't like she was making a promise she didn't intend to keep, or that he would expect something in return. If he did expect something—and he didn't seem like the creepy type who would—it wasn't anything she didn't want to give him anyway. She had already settled that matter last night, deciding to shove aside her doubts to embrace the idea of a short-term fling with someone she barely knew.

With that thought in mind, she slipped on her heels, then grabbed her purse and key card, leaving the room just as she was. Her cream bra had scrubbed out nicely, aside from a tiny red stain at the seam, and didn't show through the dress. It would work long enough for her to find Kingston and thank him properly.

Her panties grew damp at the thought of how that might progress, even though she told herself to play it cool. She intended to accept his invitation to share his bed if it was issued, and she might even make that invitation herself, but there was no reason to rush into it right this minute.

They still had the rest of the weekend, and perhaps it would be better to wait until after the wedding anyway. After all, if he rejected her overtures because she had misread him, or if the sex was terrible—a seemingly unfathomable thought—it could make the last day of the wedding awkward. Far better to have sexual tension between them than the tension of awkwardness from miscommunication or crappy sex.

She recognized a few faces from the previous evening in the foyer, but Kingston was nowhere to be found. She approached the concierge desk with a meek expression.

"Excuse me? I'm looking for Kingston Meade. I thought he would already be down here, but I don't see him. Would you mind calling his room for me?

The concierge offered a warm smile. "I can do better than that. I can escort you to see Mr. Meade now." He gestured toward the kitchen doors near the bar.

"Thank you," she replied.

She followed the concierge and slipped through the double doors, sticking close behind him as they made their way through the bustle of activity in the main kitchen to reach a smaller room in the back. It housed a walk-in refrigerator, along with another commercial-size display case holding three wedding cakes, and another one that appeared to be for a bar mitzvah. This must be a staging area for hotel event catering.

Apparently, it was also a place for handsome, generous men like Kingston to forage freely through the refrigerator apparently. She admired his audacity, almost as much she admired the trim buttocks before her, displayed so temptingly in a pair of tight jeans, as he bent down to get something from the drawer.

"Hungry?"

She looked around, half-expecting someone else to be with them in the room. "I... a little, I guess." How had he known she was there?

"Good. I hate to eat alone." A second later, he turned to face her with his arms full of food. "Even a light snack requires company to make it more pleasant, don't you think?"

She nodded as she came closer to the kitchen island where he had spread out his plundered booty. "I guess so. But how is this a little snack?"

He grinned. "I'm a big guy with a big appetite. When I'm hungry, I like to eat my fill, so the more there is, the more I love it." There was a definite sexual undertone to his words, and he underscored them by raking a lascivious glance up and down her body. It was comically exaggerated, but there was absolutely a spark of genuine lust too.

"That still seems like a lot of food. I'll see what I can do to help." She eyed the salmon, berries, and various bowls and dishes of what appeared to be leftover restaurant food. "Aren't you going to get in trouble for this?"

He paused in the middle of opening a package of honey-smoked salmon, licking his fingers before answering. "From whom? The snack police?"

She laughed. "No, I meant from the hotel. No matter how important a guest you are, surely you're not going to get away with foraging through the refrigerator?"

He winked at her. "It's my hotel, and I'll eat what I want to."

"You own the Imperial?" Wow, she no longer felt so bad about accepting the dress. He could definitely afford it, and to him, buying a designer dress had probably been something he had done without a second thought. Likely, it had never occurred to him to have his personal shopper or assistant check anywhere but an exclusive retail location. He wouldn't have even considered a chain store or an outlet mall.

He nodded. "It's one of my investment properties, and I do love the location. I live upstairs, on the top floor, and when Rafe and Breanna decided to get married, it was the perfect location for the wedding and reception." He winked at her again. "That way, I didn't have to worry about shopping for a wedding gift. I'm not good at shopping."

She looked down at the beautiful white dress. "You could've fooled me. This is an amazing dress, and even though I shouldn't take it, I really wanted to thank you for the thoughtfulness."

He resumed struggling with the salmon packet, muttering under his breath before finally tearing forcefully through the plastic with a sigh of satisfaction. "Why shouldn't you take it?" He took one of the plates from the stack on the counter, serving up a generous portion of the salmon before sliding the plate to her.

"It's an expensive dress, and we're strangers. Ethically, it's wrong to take the dress, but once I put it on, I didn't think I could take it off again."

His thoughts must have veered from food, as his gaze raked her again, pausing overly long to admire her breasts and generous hips before his eyes darted back to hers. "I hope you'll be able to take the dress off at some point, because otherwise, it's going to be incredibly difficult to fuck you."

She gasped at the bold statement. It wasn't the profanity so much as the assured confidence that they were going to get to that point. She would have called him on it, except it was completely warranted. The air sizzled with electricity from their suppressed attraction, and they both knew they wanted each other. It was only a matter of time before circumstances presented them the opportunity to act on it.

"I'm sure I can find some reason to take it off, with the

proper motivation." She licked her lips in an exaggerated fashion before taking a ripe raspberry from the package nearest to her, bringing the bright pink-red fruit to her lips and running it over the full contours before popping the berry in her mouth. It was a little too tart, and she feared her blinking eyes might have ruined the sexy moment.

He let out a low growl when he clutched the counter as though physically keeping himself from jumping across it to take her on the floor. No, apparently she hadn't ruined the sexiness of the gesture.

She picked up a bite of the salmon, taking a deep sniff of appreciation before letting the salty-sweet fish melt on her tongue. "That's delicious, but I'm really not hungry enough to enjoy it. Plus, I need a nap for tonight's activities."

"'Tonight?'" he repeated roughly, his voice thick.

She nodded, striving to look innocent. "Of course. It's Breanna's bachelorette party, and presumably Rafe's bachelor party. I imagine we'll get drunk and stare at strippers all night. Isn't that what bachelors do? And bachelorettes?"

He lifted his shoulder. "I don't know. Rafe's having a more casual get-together with just the guys."

She nodded. "Well, thanks again for the dress." With one more last swipe of her tongue across her lower lip, she pushed away from the counter and sashayed from the kitchen, practically feeling his burning gaze on her, scorching through the soft cashmere to the skin underneath. She managed to make it out of the busy kitchen before she giggled at the flirtatious interval. They knew where they were going, but the journey was just as important as the destination, and she intended to have fun along the way.

She met Breanna and several ladies downstairs in the foyer around eight o'clock that evening. To her surprise, Rafe and his friends stood nearby. Where the women had gone all out, the men looked more low-key, all wearing jeans and flannel shirts, with about half wearing leather bomber jackets, and the other half wearing light-weight wool coats. Clearly, whatever they had in mind for their evening wouldn't involve going to the club. They looked better suited for chopping wood than cutting up in a fancy nightclub.

She was running a few minutes late, so she had to hurry to catch up to the group of girls as they headed toward the exit. She had only a brief moment of eye contact with Kingston, but the desire she read in his eyes was enough to boost her confidence through the stratosphere.

She had chosen wisely, having picked out a sexy number for the bachelorette party. Though typically confident in her curves, she'd never worn anything quite as revealing as this before. The leather corset and snakeskin skirt screamed sex, or perhaps dominatrix. High-heeled gold shoes completed the look and added a few welcome inches of height to her short, curvy frame.

The bachelorette party was as clichéd as it came, but still incredibly fun. They went to a strip club as she had predicted, and hard-bodied, oiled men gyrated in a private back room for them. The g-strings they wore did little to hide the bulges pressing against the cloth, and the men flirted, touched, and behaved outrageously.

Grace was unmoved. She should have been turned on beyond belief, but instead, she was just going through the motions. Oh, she was laughing and enjoying herself with her best friend and the new girls she was becoming friendly with, but the male strippers left her cold.

All she could think about was Kingston, and discovering what he looked like underneath his lumberjack outfit. Just thinking about undoing the first few buttons of his flannel shirt was enough to make her panties drenched and cause her to shift uncomfortably in the tight leather skirt. This was a form of torture, and it was self-inflicted, because she couldn't seem to stop thinking about touching him for more than a few minutes at a time.

It was going to be a long night, especially when she was impatient to see Kingston again. All of him.

3

Kingston stared moodily into the crackling fire, his thoughts occupied with what Breanna's group might be up to at that moment. More specifically, Breanna's maid-of-honor. What was Grace doing? Was she at that moment enjoying a lap dance from some stranger, letting his cock rub up and down all over her with only a thin layer of cloth between them?

His bear rumbled in anger, and he tried to soothe it, though his heart wasn't in the task. He felt the same irrational surge of jealousy for the stripper who might or might not exist. All he knew was if he saw anything like that, some dancer rubbing against his mate, he'd probably tear the man in half before turning to Grace to remind her to whom she belonged.

Which was completely unfair, since she didn't know she belonged to him. Of course she had free will to reject him too, and as a human, she wasn't as bound by her pheromones as he was. She wouldn't recognize him as her mate just by scent, and she was quite likely to freak out if and when he told her about his ursine side.

Cold, hard facts didn't make him feel any better about imagining strange men groping her curvy frame. Just thinking about her skin pressed into that sexy leather outfit she wore earlier made his cock ache and renewed his hard-on all over again. Not that the damn thing had ceased to be a nuisance at all since he'd seen her like that. That black corset thing and red skirt had nearly been enough to make him lose complete control of his bear.

The animal inside had roared at him to pick her up and spirit her away somewhere private, where they could claim her as theirs. He wanted to sink into the slick well between her thick thighs as much as he wanted to bite her, to mark her with his pheromones and let all other male bear-shifters know she was off-limits.

Having to wait was killing him, but it wouldn't be fair to Rafe to cause drama at his wedding, and it wouldn't be fair to overwhelm Grace with the knowledge that he was Ursus sapien instead of Homo sapien. He doubted Breanna had enlightened Grace, so when he told her he could shift to a polar bear, she was unlikely to take the news well, at least at first.

It was advisable to have a strong relationship building between them before he revealed that side. He'd never met a woman he thought was his mate before, but he'd had a few serious relationships in the past, and the one human to whom he had revealed the truth had never spoken to him again. She had been terrified enough to quit her high-paying job and move across the country.

He had been saddened by the loss of her and had cared enough to make sure she had settled safely with discreet inquiries, rather than approaching her himself, but he'd also learned that he shouldn't reveal all of himself until he was certain his next partner was secure in the relationship, and was open-minded enough to give the bear side of him a chance.

Kingston prided himself in his impeccable sense of self-control, but Grace presented a unique challenge. With her, his control seemed to vanish into thin air. He didn't think he could hold back long enough to have the shifter talk before burying himself deep inside her and taking her, hard and deep, and making her come again and again and again.

But on one point Kingston was certain — he wouldn't truly mate with a woman until she knew what he was. He wouldn't bite her or mark her as his, not until she knew about and accepted his shifter nature.

"You look lost in thought," said Rafe as he sat on the log near him. Both men had stripped down to just jeans, and the crackling bonfire provided ample warmth when coupled with the revved-up metabolism of a shifter. Their bears were eager to shed the human form and run and hunt in this private retreat, but they were all waiting until a few beers had made them mellow before unleashing the animals inside. The other men were all shifters too, and their idea of a bachelor party was to come out to the woods and take down the elk Kingston had flown in just for the occasion.

He shrugged. "It's nothing."

"Is nothing about five-four, with heavenly curves, and also my mate's best friend?"

Kingston smiled, allowing that to be his answer as he tossed a handful of twigs into the fire. "Let's do this thing."

"Hell yeah," said Rafe. "I don't get how Breanna can prefer a group of half-dressed men to coming out into nature."

"It's because she's a human, and not a bear. If she had

one, her inner bear would be telling her to join us." He frowned slightly. "Don't you have a problem with your fiancée going to a strip club?"

Rafe shook his head. "Nah. She'll be thinking of me the whole time. It wasn't her idea anyway. One of the girls from her job came up with the plan, and she just went along with it since it's the typical bachelorette routine."

"Well I don't like it," said Kingston, realizing he sounded like a petulant child even to himself. "It's not proper."

Rafe laughed heartily. "Which is why it's a bachelorette party and not afternoon tea, my friend." He clapped him on the shoulders. "Besides, I don't think you have anything to worry about."

He frowned at his friend. "We were talking about your mate."

Rafe laughed again, shaking his head. "No, I think we were talking about yours."

Strangely, he felt embarrassed, and a hint of heat crept into his cheeks. "I don't have a mate."

"I think you will soon. You recognized her, didn't you? I mean her pheromones don't smell all that special to me, but Breanna's my whole world. I just recognized the look when you first saw her the other night."

He didn't bother to deny it as he shucked off his shoes and jeans, stretching for a moment before allowing the polar bear inside to spring free. Yes, he had recognized that she would fit together with him perfectly the very first night he'd met her. Was it just last night? It seemed like much longer. He'd thought she was the one when he sat down beside her, but when her arousal had thickened the air with her unique perfume, he had *known*.

Well, his bear had known, and the animal had roared to snatch her up in his arms and flee the rehearsal dinner so they could to go somewhere quiet to mate. His bear wanted him to mark her right then, and the human side had only put up token resistance, completely fueled solely by propriety.

He wasn't resistant to finding a mate, and he was actually looking forward to making that match. Unlike his friend Rafe—who had changed his mind since meeting Breanna—he had always believed bears could recognize the mate meant for them, or at least one who would be an ideally suited match. He didn't know if it was a biological imperative, or perhaps a bear's senses that told him the mate for him would be a genetically compatible match to ensure offspring, or if it was something more mystical. All he knew was he believed in it, and he had began to despair that he would ever find his mate as he approached thirty-six.

That fear was alleviated, but completely supplanted by a new one—fear that Grace wouldn't want him when she knew all about him, and that she would run away as Suzanne had all those years ago. When he lost Suzanne, it had caused heartache that had dissipated slowly over a period of weeks. He had a feeling losing Grace would be far worse, and he hadn't even officially had her yet.

As he broke into a loping run alongside his brethren, he vowed that would change as soon as possible. With any luck, maybe even tonight.

―――――

His hunt had done little to distract him from thoughts of his mate, and he couldn't resist the urge to detour to her floor when they arrived back at the hotel a few hours later. He had asked the front desk which room she was in earlier, ostensibly to know where to deliver the dress, but in actuality with this shadowy plan in mind.

He didn't want to frighten her or scare her away, so he knocked with some trepidation on her door. He braced himself for rejection, determined he would leave the moment she told him to, or if she even seemed hesitant at all about him being there. The last thing he wanted to do was make her think he was some psycho obsessed with her.

He could see himself becoming obsessed, but not in a psychotic fashion. It wouldn't take much for all of his thoughts to revolve around her though, and for her to fit easily into his life simply because he would be determined to make her fit. It was too soon to talk about such things with her though, so he had to content himself with moving slower than that and with whatever was offered tonight, if anything.

She opened the door a moment later, and he barely bit back a groan. At first glance, she wore a granny nightgown that covered her from head to toe. A second look revealed it was made of some kind of diaphanous yellow material that showed far more than it hid. It was a juxtaposition of demure and sexy, and she wore it well. Of course, he'd prefer she not be wearing anything at all.

If she was surprised to see him, it didn't show. "Kingston," she said with a purr. If her pheromones hadn't revealed she was completely human, he would've sworn she was a cat-shifter from the way she drew out his name and arched her body.

"Grace." He loved the sound of her name on his lips. It was a single syllable, but strong yet feminine, just like her. "I was thinking about you."

"So was I. Thinking about you, I mean," she purred again. And then she giggled as she ran a hand down her belly, pausing an inch or so above her mound. "I was just thinking about thinking about you while I touch myself. I was thinking if that would be bad to do that again, or if I would come just as hard as I did last night doing that. Thinking about you, I mean. Which I'm thinking about thinking about doing." She dissolved into giggles.

He groaned softly, recognizing the signs of inebriation. Dammit, there went his plans for the night. She seemed open and receptive, and he didn't doubt he could be between her thighs in a short amount of time if he invited himself in, but it wouldn't be right with her in this state. Instead, he pushed away from the doorjamb he'd leaned against with a sigh. "I just wanted to tell you good night."

Her face fell. "That's it? Are you sure don't want to come in for a drink...or something?"

He shook his head. "I wouldn't say no to a goodnight kiss," he said in a thick whisper. His bear was chomping at the bit to pin her to the wall and take her, but he was trying to rein in the impulse. It was going to be hard enough just to confine it to a simple kiss, but he couldn't imagine leaving without tasting those full, luscious lips.

She licked them as she leaned closer, wrapping her hands around the lapels of his leather jacket to drag him closer. He stepped forward to meet her, putting his arms around her soft frame and relishing having her so near him.

Her softness cuddled his hardness to perfection, and she was the perfect counterpart to him. He couldn't have designed a more ideal female if he'd had a computer program in front of him with an unlimited amount of choices. His bear had known from the start, and holding her like this as his mouth touched hers reinforced the knowledge to the man. Grace was his mate, and eventually—no, soon—he would claim her as such.

Her lips were soft against his, and he started the kiss gently and with good intentions. When he would have stepped back, she whimpered and pulled him closer, deepening the kiss. Kingston pushed his tongue inside her mouth, anxious to taste every bit of her. His enhanced senses savored her flavor and her aroma, and he deepened the kiss further as his hands moved lower. Cupping her generous buttocks, he kneaded them gently as he lifted her against him, so the apex of her thighs cradled his hardened erection.

He groaned softly when she rubbed against him, teasing him with how it would be when there were no clothes separating them. He wanted to give up control, to surrender to his bear's urge to take her now, but he remembered she wasn't completely aware. Alcohol had robbed her of some level of inhibition, and it wouldn't be right to use this current state against her. When she came to his bed, he wanted to make sure it was completely willing and with no ambiguity about choice or decisions. Because once he had her, he didn't think he could ever let her go.

With that thought in mind, he pushed himself away from her, slowly disengaging by weakening the intensity of the kiss before unwrapping her arms around his body, guiding hers to her side as he stepped back. "Good night, Grace."

She looked disgruntled, but didn't argue as he stepped into the hallway and turned away from her. A glance back revealed she was touching her lips, her expression somewhere between dazed and annoyed, with a strong note of passion.

It was some consolation to know she would go to bed equally frustrated, though the alcohol would probably put her out much faster. He was not looking forward to the sleepless night ahead of him, and he doubted a quick jerk-off would be enough to allow him to sleep or clear his senses from the overload of having almost been intimate with his mate.

Sometimes, it sucked to do the right thing.

4

The wedding was beautiful, and seeing Rafe and Breanna kiss so tenderly after their heartfelt exchange of vows caused a thick lump to form in her throat. Grace cleared it as she dabbed discreetly at her eyes with the lace handkerchief that was part of the bouquets, cleverly draping them to hide the ends of the flowers. It had been a beautiful ceremony, and she didn't doubt the sincerity as they had traded words of love and commitment. She knew with absolute certainty that Breanna and Rafe would be together for life.

The thought sent her gaze skittering toward Kingston, and she wasn't surprised to find him staring at her. Their gazes locked, and her heart rate accelerated as her panties dampened. Thanks to an excess of Jell-O shots and margaritas, she was a little hazy about last night, but she certainly remembered the intense kiss they had shared. If Kingston had pressed to come in last night, she would not only have opened the door wide with welcoming arms, she would have tossed him on the bed and climbed on top.

In the fresh light of sobriety, nothing had changed. She

smiled softly at him, taking a moment to lick her lips in an exaggerated fashion before winking at him as Rafe and Breanna turned to meet their guests as Mr. and Mrs. Cabello.

A second later, her arm entwined with Kingston's, and they walked down the aisle behind the happy couple. Most of the ceremony had passed in a blur, and the reception was the same way. She did all the things expected of her, including making a speech, but her thoughts were solely dedicated to Kingston, and determining a way to make sure tonight didn't end with a panty-melting kiss but nothing else. She was due to fly home the day after tomorrow, so she wanted to take full advantage of the short time remaining to indulge in her casual fling.

A pang went to her at the thought of it being just a fling, and she tried to push away that reaction. She was trying something new here, attempting a physical relationship without letting her emotions get entangled—or at least too entangled. They were already slightly muddled, and she didn't think she was imagining that he felt the same way.

That was no guarantee there would be anything more than sex between them, and she wanted to have realistic expectations. She wanted to look back on her brief time with Kingston with fondness and nostalgia, perhaps a bit of longing for it again, not with regret or a broken heart.

It seemed to take forever to get through the round of speeches, the dinner, and the dancing. She was happy for Breanna's happiness, but she couldn't wait for the beautiful wedding to end so she could approach Kingston.

Not that she hadn't tried a few times during the reception. Every time she made the effort to get close to him, Ashley had been there to cock-block her. She didn't know if cock-block was the correct term, since neither of them had cocks, but it was the same principle. There was something deeply disturbed about the chick, and she had made it her mission to keep Grace and Kingston apart.

With a start, she realized all the single women were gathering to catch the bouquet. That meant the reception was nearly over—or at least the part for which she had to stay. Once Rafe and Breanna slipped away to take his helicopter to their mountain cabin in the Coeur d'Alene Mountains for their honeymoon, she could also slip away, hopefully with Kingston beside her.

She joined the single ladies in the crowd, but not really making an effort to catch the bouquet. Apparently, Breanna had other ideas, because her friend made a production of putting a hand over her eyes before tossing the bouquet, but she moved her hand at the last minute and winked at Grace when she threw the bouquet directly at her.

It should have landed easily in her hands, but a sharp shove from the right sent her flying out of the way and careening across the room, where she landed with a sharp jarring thud against the marble floor. The collision knocked the wind out of her, and it took a moment to realize Ashley had physically shoved her out of the way to snatch the bouquet in midflight. Shocked silence greeted the other woman's actions for a moment, even as she pirouetted with delight, crowing about her victory.

Ashley's gaze was firmly on Kingston as he made his way through the crowd, and apparently the silly woman thought he was coming to declare his love or something. Her eyes shone with excitement, which faded to dull disappointment a moment later when he turned away from her and knelt beside Grace, who barely bit back a grin of triumph. She didn't normally go for mean-girl games, but it was quite satisfying to know Ashley's dreams had just turned to dust when he chose the chubby girl over her. It wasn't a shock to anyone else, but clearly, Ashley had failed to realize she wasn't even in the running.

Her thoughts fled from the pale woman a moment later as Kingston lifted her into his arms. She gasped with shock, instinctively curling her arm around his shoulders, the other clutching the lapels of his tuxedo. No man had carried her before, and he made it seem effortless, though she briefly considered protesting. Deciding that would make it more awkward than if she just pretended as though men carried her everywhere every day, she curled against him and let him take her from the ballroom where they'd held the reception.

As they neared the elevator, she squirmed to get down. "I can walk."

"Yes, you can, but now that I have you in my arms, I'm not letting go until I put you down on my bed."

She arched a brow at that and was surprised when he veered away from the elevator bank toward the exit. "What are you doing?"

"I'm taking you somewhere special."

A moment later, a sleek black sports car appeared out front, and a valet attendant got out to hand him the keys. In a move that should have been awkward, but he managed to make smooth, Kingston bent down and settled her into the passenger seat, going so far as to buckle her in before slamming her door.

A moment later, he entered through the driver side and settled onto the luxurious leather seat. "I had to put you down temporarily." He pulled a face. "It just sounded far more romantic the other way."

She giggled. "I don't think you have to worry about lacking in the romance department. That whole *Officer and*

Gentleman thing, where you carried me out of the hotel? That was pretty damned romantic."

He grinned. "I'm glad to hear it. I hope I suitably impressed you and put you in a state of mind where you don't object to being ravished all night long?"

She tilted her head, pretending to think about it for a moment. "You expect me to endure an entire night of sex with you, our hands and mouths roaming freely, our bodies joined together as we fuck with animal lust?" She barely held back a groan of desire at the thought. "You might have to carry me a bit more first."

He laughed with gusto. "If that's the payoff, I'll gladly care you for the rest of my life, love."

The words took her breath, but she wasn't sure if it was in a good or a bad way. They sparked hope in her, but it could be could be an irrational hope. It was the kind of throwaway line a man might use on a woman he wanted to get in bed, but wanted nothing permanent with, and she had to remind herself of that sternly. Answers in the heat of the moment didn't always reflect how a person really felt, and she couldn't read more into it than he actually meant.

"Now, that's okay. I mostly prefer to walk and stand on my own two feet, but the novelty of being carried was nice."

"It shouldn't be a novelty, and I'll be happy to do it any time."

He drove smoothly through the Seattle traffic, taking them to the marina. He entered a private section a few minutes later, and urged her to stay in the car.

She assumed he was going for something, so it was a bit of a surprise to have him open her door and lift her out a moment later once he'd disengaged her seatbelt. "I can walk, you know. It wasn't like that catty she-bitch actually hurt me when she shoved me down." A slight throbbing in her ankle disagreed, but it wasn't anything serious, and she certainly could walk on her own.

"I'm sweeping you off your feet, so be quiet and enjoy it." He winked at her, which soothed the urge to protest the command. His lighthearted teasing was far different than if he had been seriously telling her to be quiet.

Deciding to take his good advice, she shut her mouth and curled against him, arm around his neck again as he strode to a small yacht. He walked up the gangplank confidently, and a man in a white uniform appeared a moment later.

"Good evening, sir. We didn't expect to see you again until next weekend."

"It was a last-minute change of plans, Skipper. We'd like to go to my island please."

If the man was put out at being forced to take the boat out this late at night, well after nine p.m., he showed no signs of it. Apparently, he was paid well to follow his employer's whims without protest.

True to his word, Kingston didn't set her down when he took her below deck. They had a beautiful view of the water, but it was enclosed in glass to protect them from the cold night air, and she enjoyed the view seated on his lap, head tucked against his shoulder. The waves moved the boat gently, but it was barely noticeable, either because the boat was large enough, or the water was calm enough. As they moved from the bay into the Strait of Juan de Fuca, his hand moved from the outside of her thigh to the top and inside.

She held her breath as his fingers trailed up her thigh, reaching the hem of her dress and slipping under it. They continued their upward assent until reaching the tiny silk panties she wore. She bit her lip as Kingston's finger penetrated the elastic side and brushed lightly against her neatly trimmed mound. She couldn't help a small groan when he pressed against her clit before moving his fingers lower, two of them pressing gently into her opening that was slick with need.

"Mine," he said with his low growl. "I've been waiting for this honey cache for what seems like forever."

She trembled as his fingers slid deeper inside her, pressing in and out of her slowly as his thumb began to circle her clitoris. "We've only known each other a couple of days," she said amid breathless pants. Her hips acted of their own accord, rising to meet each stroke of his fingers.

"It seems much longer that I've been waiting for my mate."

Her eyes widened, but she wasn't certain if it was from the orgasm that swept over her unexpectedly or his puzzling words. Did he mean she was his mate? Was he envisioning a future between them, or was she deluding herself?

Pleasure pushed away all thought, sweeping it aside in a tide of ecstasy as he continued to stroke and touch her, not letting her off his lap or away from him for the next hour. When he wasn't actively stroking her, his fingers stayed buried inside her folds, and he would periodically pluck another orgasm from her.

Several times, she made the attempt to reciprocate, but he held her firmly on his lap, and at his mercy, giving her pleasure over and over.

It was almost a relief for the boat to draw up to the dock finally, forcing his hand to move from between her thighs. He still didn't let her up as he brought his hand to his nose, inhaling deeply, his eyes closing as he savored her scent.

A moment later, he licked her essence from his fingers, sending a new rush of arousal through her, much to her chagrin. She should be unable to get turned on again after four orgasms and constant stimulation, but she was already ready for another one—but she wanted him along for the ride this time, his large cock seated fully inside her.

She didn't know he was large for certain, since he hadn't let her touch it, but sitting on his lap had afforded her a unique perspective and led her to believe he was generously endowed. Two of his fingers had made her feel more filled than any lover she could recall, so she couldn't wait to see what he could do with his manhood.

The dock was part of a large structure with winding stairs that led to a house up on a bluff. The stairs were a special kind of torture when all she wanted to do was drop down and let him fuck her, but he made it easier by carrying her up them. At least his hands were busy that way, and he couldn't continue the sensual torture that kept her in such a state on the boat ride to his island.

"This place is amazing," she said when they finally reached the top step five minutes later. He wasn't even winded, and he'd carried her the entire way up the sharp incline of stairs. It boded well for his stamina, and she was certain she could look forward to a long night, but the best kind of long night in a good way.

"Yes, it is. I don't mind the city, and it's easier to conduct business there, but I spend most of my weekends and free time here. This is where we had Rafe's bachelor party."

She wrinkled her nose. "Did you have a bunch of dancers boated in for the occasion?"

He laughed softly. "No, we abstained from strippers, unlike you wild girls. Instead, we had a bonfire and some drinking, followed by an elk hunt."

She arched her brow. "How very rugged and manly of you."

His half-grin was all sexy. "I like to think so. I'm looking forward to showing you just how rugged and manly I can be."

"I'm looking forward to that too. You can put me down now if you want."

He shook his head. "I already told you I'm not letting you down until I get to my bed. With a couple of brief exceptions, that's still true."

She could argue about it, or she could give in and get there that much faster. With a sigh of satisfaction, she melted against him. "Then hurry up and get me there, because I can't wait to see what you're hiding under that tuxedo." The house was designed along the lines of a log cabin, but with an unlimited budget, and it was clear no expense had been spared.

He whisked her quickly through the rooms, not bothering to give her a tour as he took her up yet another flight of stairs to his room, before kicking open the door and crossing the room to lay her on the bed. She had little time to process anything as he was soon beside her again, his hands moving frantically, but with finesse, as he eased the purple and gold gown from her body. She was glad he hadn't ripped it, because it was the most beautiful one she owned aside from the cashmere dress he had given her.

A moment later, he stood up to shed his clothes, and she watched each piece of clothing fall off, revealing his magnificent body a section at a time. Her mouth watered, and her pussy was slick with need by the time he had shed everything and returned to the bed.

He was even better endowed than she had guessed, his underwear clearly straining hard to confine the large cock between his legs. Her mouth watered at the sight of him shucking his underwear, and she reached out a hand to wrap around his shaft, pumping lightly. He swelled in her palm, twitching as she stroked him before scooting down the bed and bending her head to close her mouth over him.

She had to stretch her mouth to the point of making her jaw ache to accommodate him, but it was a good stretch, made even better by his groan of pure male satisfaction as she began to bob her head, licking and sucking on his manhood.

His hands were busy as well, cupping her breasts and stroking her body, as his mouth occupied itself uttering sounds pleasure.

As she worked the length of him, pressing slick folds against his bare leg in a search for relief from the arousal burning through her, he started to twitch. A second later, Kingston pushed her forcefully away and flipped her onto her stomach. She giggled as he moved behind her, lifting her ass into the air and holding her hips with his hands. He'd lost his smooth edge in his frantic motions, and she reveled in seeing his loss of control, which mimicked her own.

"Are you protected?" He growled the words thickly, sounding more animal than human in his passion.

She nodded jerkily. "I'm clean too. You?"

"Yes," he said with another deep rumble as the head of his cock pressed into her entrance. With no resistance due to all the liquid heat generated by her arousal, he surged inside, going balls-deep on the first thrust.

He was as large as she'd expected, and even more, but it felt so good that she howled her pleasure as she arched backward to meet his animalistic thrusts, both of them driven by need rather than control

They made love forcefully and intensely, and she lost track of how many times she came as he thrust inside her.

She was certain Kingston came at least once, pausing very briefly before continuing his passionate onslaught.

Eventually, satisfaction drove away the frantic edge of passion, and the collapsed together in an exhausted heap on the bed. She wanted to speak, though she wasn't sure what to say. In the end, she surrendered to the wave of lethargy sweeping over her, deciding they could talk more in the morning. For now, their bodies had already said everything they needed to say tonight.

5

To her surprise, she woke before him. It was tempting to wake him up and indulge in another round of lovemaking, but he looked so peaceful sleeping she couldn't bear to wake him just yet. Instead, a cup of coffee beckoned, as did her morning walk. She had nothing truly suitable for a morning walk, but she borrowed one of his flannel shirts, which hung down to her knees, and a pair of boots she found in the mud room. They were way too big, but they would be all right for a short walk. She just needed to get outside and clear her head.

Deciding to walk and then have coffee, she slipped from the house after shrugging on his jacket. It was a new experience to feel like a little kid dressed in adult clothes, since hers were usually purchased in the plus-size department. She liked the idea of wearing her boyfriend's flannel shirt, and she grinned to herself as she stepped off the back stairs and wandered slowly down the path to the bluff.

Was he her boyfriend? It was a presumptuous assumption, but somewhere in the middle of the night, she clearly recalled him rolling her over, pinning her to the bed, teasing her to near climax, but then refusing to enter her until she admitted she belonged to him, and he was allowed to keep her.

A soft smile curved her lips at the memory, but morning light brought an unwelcome dose of doubt. Was he sincere, or had it been pillow talk in the middle of the night, in the midst of passion? She thought he had been genuine, but she didn't want to pin her hopes on something that might not be real.

Startlingly enough for her, she realized it was real on her side. It wouldn't take much for her to fall completely head-over-heels in love with Kingston, and if he wanted her to stay with him, she would. She would happily uproot her life in Calgary and move to Seattle to be with him, if he truly wanted that.

Could she fell in love with someone in the space of a weekend? It seemed ridiculous, but she was already experiencing a very strong case of almost-love, coupled with the feverish state of urgent lust. She couldn't get enough of him, and if he felt the same way, why should they waste time that was too precious just to follow a more conventional progression of their romance?

She crested the hill, and the view took her breath away, while detracting her thoughts. The Strait stretched out before her, and she could see a few tiny islands nearby, but they were vague, misty shapes in the fog. The ocean crashed against the beach down below, and while beautiful, the water looked tumultuous and scary, even from a distance.

Still, she was compelled to move closer to the short fence guarding the edge of the bluff. She was glad whomever had designed the railing had gone with an unobtrusive, short style that allowed one to fully enjoy the view. As she turned to admire another angle, a flash of white caught her eyes. Abandoning the view, Grace looked in that direction and froze at the sight of a large white cat near her.

Cat wasn't the right word. Mountain lion, bobcat, or maybe a panther? She'd never seen a white panther before, and she had the strangest thought that it looked just like Ashley, especially with its pale blue eyes. It was a stunningly beautiful animal, but she didn't want to get any closer.

Unfortunately, the animal didn't share her urge to shy away apparently, because it stalked toward her with a predatory air. She stumbled backward, anxious to put distance between herself and the cat, wishing she hadn't taken Kingston's boots. Her bare feet would be preferable for running, and she started to kick off the boots to prepare herself should the need arise.

The cat growled at her, a fearsome sound that raised the hair on the nape of her neck and made her scream. "Help. Help, Kingston. Help me."

The cat darted toward her, stopping just a few inches before her as it leapt with perfect grace. Looking at the animal, meeting its eyes, Grace had the strangest feeling it was toying with her.

Finally, her second foot came free of the boot, and she turned and ran in earnest. It didn't take long to realize she had run the wrong way, and she was rapidly running out of ground. The short wooden fence was growing ever closer, as was the steep drop over the bluff, and she skidded to a halt about two inches before ramming into it.

Hoping against hope that the panther had veered away, she turned around and wasn't surprised to see the creature just a few feet from her, stalking slowly forward. The damned thing was definitely playing with her, which was an insane notion, but she couldn't deny the intelligence in its eyes. And maliciousness.

No, wild animals wouldn't be malicious. She was letting fear carry away her imagination.

Suddenly, the cat's ears perked, and it let out a low hissing sound as it looked over its shoulder. Grace didn't know what had gotten the panther's attention, but she hoped to see Kingston standing there with a large gun. When she looked that way, she saw nothing, and the moment she looked back at the panther, it was just in time to see the cat spring at her.

She flailed to evade the claw that tried to rake down her chest and shoulder, falling backward as she did so. The fence did nothing to stop her descent, and she tumbled right over it, off the bluff, and toward the icy water below.

Fear must really have a hold on her, because when she looked up as she started to scream, she swore she saw the panther shift into the smug form of Ashley, staring down at her with a satisfied smirk. When she blinked, the cat and the Ashley apparition were both gone, but the water was coming ever closer. She curled into a ball and braced herself for the impact, remembering as she hit the water that it would have been better to point her feet downward to make less of a splash and minimize the impact.

The water hit with a bone-jarring thud, and the cold immediately overtook her. Shock and pain rendered her unable to move, and she opened her mouth to take in a breath without thought. Water flooded into her nose and mouth, creating panic.

She flailed wildly, knowing she was going to die in this cold water, and Kingston wouldn't even realize she was gone for a while yet. Would they even find her body, or would she should be listed officially as a missing person, never to be found? She hoped they wouldn't think Kingston had killed her.

Suddenly a shape caught her attention, but she was still too panicked to really take it in. Her frazzled brain processed it as long and white, and she was convinced for a second the panther had come to finish the job.

Instead, the animal folded her in a large paw and cradled her against its white chest, holding her securely even through her violent coughing as it swam with surety toward the surface. Seconds later, they were out of the water and on the rocky beach below the bluff. He laid her down on her side. She continued coughing until her lungs finally seemed clear of water, then propped herself up on her elbows with a weak moan.

She stared in disbelief at the polar bear shaking off near her. What was it doing this far south? More importantly, why had it rescued her? Or had it simply captured her, planning to make her its next meal?

She let out a bleat of terror when the bear started to look sort of fuzzy, shifting out of focus for a moment. At first, she assumed it was a head injury, though she hadn't bumped her head that she recalled. Seconds later, the fuzziness sharpened, but it was no longer a bear sitting on the beach in front of her. Instead, Kingston sat there, looking concerned and wary.

She stared at him, unable to take in what she was seeing. It penetrated her mind, even in her fuzzy haze, that he was completely naked. That made sense, she supposed. It would be difficult to turn into a polar bear with your clothes on. The idea was laughably insane, and she started to giggle. It didn't take long for hysteria to take over, making her collapse into a heap on the beach even though she wanted to get up and leave. Her half-frozen limbs refused her urges to move.

"Are you all right?" he asked with a wary note in his voice, as though he expected her to run away screaming.

"Nope," she said distinctly as she continued to giggle, the laughter taking on a shrill edge that betrayed the fear and shock underneath. "I'm about as not okay as you can get, Kingston. What the hell is happening?"

"I can explain."

Her teeth started chattering, and her entire body shook with shivers. The icy water seemed to have seeped all the way to her bones, and she didn't think she would ever be warm again. "Then do so," she said through chattering teeth that distorted her words.

He made an impatient sound and came closer. Grace tried to flinch away from him, but he wouldn't be deterred as he lifted her into his arms. "How do we get back up there?" It was an inane question, but she couldn't seem to focus on or process anything too taxing at the moment.

"The stairs," he said grimly, setting off in that direction. By the time he had mounted all the stairs and taken her back to his house, she was freezing and literally couldn't move. Numbness had settled in her extremities, and she didn't know if it was frostbite or just plain old shock, coupled with some lingering injury from hitting the water with such force.

He sat her on a rocking chair near the fire, and she started to take a blanket from the back of it.

"You need to get undressed first," he said gruffly.

She shook her head. "No way." Who knew when she might need to flee for her life—as soon as she could move that was?

He scowled at her before turning to toss wood into the fireplace, his irritation clear as he bent to fuss with the kindling. "You might have hypothermia, and it will just get worse and make it that much harder to get warm if you stay in those wet clothes. I'm not going to hurt you, and I'm not going to jump on you, so take off your damn clothing before you get under the blanket."

She glared at his back, not appreciating his tone, but allowing common sense to sway her. Unfortunately, her fingers refused to cooperate, and she ended up sitting in the chair, a huddled, frozen mess.

When he turned from the crackling fire a moment later and saw her still dressed, he sighed with impatience. "Would you really rather die than take your clothes off around me again?"

She rolled her eyes. "I tried. My fingers won't work." Her teeth were still chattering, and her words were still somewhat incomprehensible, but he seemed to be able to make them out.

His touch was tender as he undressed her, but with an air of aloofness that suggested he was focused solely on getting her warm, and not on sexual pleasure.

It was only after she was curled in front of the fire, wrapped in three blankets, and her fingers finally started to move properly, that she was able to broach the subject of what she had seen. "I was hallucinating, wasn't I?" There was a hint of desperation in her words as she silently begged him to lie to her.

His lips tightened, and he shook his head. "No, you weren't hallucinating. I'm a bear-shifter, Grace, and Ashley is a panther-shifter."

Her eyes widened. "Ashley was the one who attacked me?" It sounded insane just saying it, but she accepted the truth immediately. She had realized the big cat was toying with her, and she'd also noticed strange resemblance to the woman who had been such an annoying nuisance the past few days. Still, it was quite a step up from spilling wine and nasty insults to trying to kill someone. "But why me?"

"Because she knows I've found my mate, but she thinks if she gets rid of you, I'll turn to her. Shifters often take mates without finding the one truly meant for them, because no one likes to be alone, but she's insane if she thinks I could ever settle for anything like that after having been with you last night."

Grace stared at him in openmouthed shock, unable to decide what to address first. Was he serious? "You think I'm your *mate*? How the hell does that work?"

His lip curled slightly, but his tone was almost academic when he answered. "Our best guess is a biological connection. The animal inside recognizes compatible genetics through pheromone matching. Some shifters don't even believe in instantly recognizing your mate, but I always did, and the night I met you, I just knew you were mine."

Her eyes widened with fear. "What does being your mate mean? I don't understand. Are you going to lock me away somewhere?"

He gave a harsh bark of laughter that held little amusement. "No, I'm not going to keep you prisoner, Grace. You have the choice to decline me, and it's much easier for you as a human. You aren't influenced by extra senses, and you can't smell my pheromones that may sway you to make a decision you don't want to make. If you want to walk away, there's not a damn thing I can do about it, and I certainly won't try to stop you."

She licked her lips, her head whirling. "This is just so much to take in. I half-think I just hit my head really hard, but I don't remember colliding with anything."

Kingston snorted. "If you're having trouble believing

your senses, talk to Breanna. She'll confirm what I'm telling you."

Her eyes widened, and she shook her head automatically. "There's no way Breanna is a shifter...person...thingy. I would know, because I lived with her for two years as her roommate."

Kingston sighed loudly, clearly irritated. "Breanna isn't a shifter, but Rafe is. He turns into a grizzly bear, while I'm a polar bear. We met in Alaska one summer on a salmon-fishing trip."

"In your bear forms?" It was a stupid question, but she couldn't seem to help uttering those as she tried to take in everything he was saying.

Kingston grinned. "Occasionally, but we met on an official guided tour, and it was a summer trip from both our parents to celebrate our high school graduations."

She cocked a brow. "Don't most people go to Europe or something for that kind of trip?" Her parents hadn't been in the tax bracket that allowed such indulgences, so she didn't truly know.

He shrugged. "Shifters need to be back in nature on a regular basis. We're not happy if we aren't."

"Do your parents live at the North Pole?"

He laughed again, looking amused rather than offended. "Honey, we're human too. You're Homo sapien, and I'm Ursus sapiens, which gives us a few distinct physiological traits, but we're not all living on the polar ice caps and hunting seals. We've adapted to live among Homo sapiens, and my family has lived in Seattle and the surrounding area for more than a hundred years. Rafe's family is in Oregon, but he moved here after college so we could go into business together."

"Let me make sure I have this straight. First of all, my

best friend is now married to a grizzly bear, his best man is a polar bear, with whom I just spent an entirely amazing night, and I'm on some panther's hit list because you think I'm your mate?" Uttering it aloud didn't make it sound any less preposterous, but for some reason, she found his matter-of-fact nod reassuring. "That all sounds completely nuts."

Kingston laughed softly. "I know, and I wanted to wait a while longer before I told you, before I made you my mate completely, but Ashley has accelerated the timeline of events."

"I'm still not entirely sure what this whole mate thing means?"

"Bear-shifters usually mate for life, Grace. This is one bear who plans to, and if you'll have me, I'll be the happiest man *and* bear around. It's like being my wife, but in our culture, it's called a mate. We can still do all the legal trappings of the human world, just like Rafe and Breanna, but mating is sealed just between you and me. It involves me biting you lightly on a regular basis to impart my pheromones onto yours, which is a way to protect you."

She scowled. "You're going to bite me to protect me? Am I going to turn me into a bear-shifter?"

He sighed raggedly. "No. We're distinct species, and there's no way to transfer your traits to me or vice versa."

"What about children?"

His expression softened. "I'd love to have several cubs with you, but I don't want to do that right away. I'd like to enjoy some time with just you and me for a while first."

Was the perfect answer, except the *cubs* things scared the hell out of her. "Cubs, as in actual cubs?"

He shook his head. "They'll be born looking as human as you, my darling, and the bear-shifter traits will come later, along with puberty. We suspect it's a latent gene triggered by hormonal changes, but there aren't exactly a huge group of bear-shifter scientists available to investigate our unique biology."

She nodded, accepting the logic with equanimity. It was amazing how quickly her mind was starting to adapt and come around to everything that had happened this morning, and everything she had learned. She was still frightened, but not of Kingston. He was gentle, even when he was being a bit gruff and bossy, and she knew instinctively he would never hurt her. In fact, he had saved her life from that crazy Ashley—which reminded her. "What are you going to do about Ashley? She's not going to like us mating, and I'm not going to live in fear of that crazy cat."

His eyes sparkled with hope at her words, but he addressed her question. "We have our own justice system, and she'll be answering to them. Most likely, she'll be banished to a preserve somewhere, shunned from polite society, and forced to live with either other shifter criminals or perhaps pure panthers. Whatever happens to her, she deserves it."

Grace nodded, feeling not an iota of sympathy for the other woman's predicament. The crazy bitch couldn't live among civilized people if she was going to go homicidal. "Well, in that case, if you're certain you'll be dealing with her, I think I'd like to stick around for a while."

He nodded. "We'll handle Ashley. I'll hired additional security for now, and it shouldn't take long to track her down."

"You have trackers in your world?"

He nodded. "Like the police in human society, I guess. Now, may we change the subject to a more interesting topic?"

"What did you have in mind?" The peek downward at his burgeoning erection revealed exactly what he had in mind. "I'm open to all topics of discussion."

"Good." He said it with a growl, as he leaned closer to pluck her from her spot on the floor and settle her on his lap. Her blankets fell in the process, but she was amply warmed by that time, especially when his arms settled around her, imparting the heat of his body.

She ran her hands down his chest, smiling slightly. "For a bear, you're not very hairy."

He laughed. "I'm not very hairy for a human either, but I hope that's okay?"

She grinned before nodding. "That's fine. It's not the hair that makes the bear, or something like that." Her voice turned sultry as her hand drifted lower to stroke his cock. "Maybe it's something to do with the size of your erection making the bear? If so, your name is apt. This guy is king-sized."

"If you keep that up, you might meet my inner bear."

"You don't mean to... While we're..." She couldn't hide a shudder of distaste at the thought.

His arms tightened around her, and he growled again. "Of course not. I have excellent control over my bear, and I would never shift in the middle of being intimate with you. I rarely shift except on weekends when I come here to the island, so you might get glances of me pawing around in my bear form, but whenever we interact, I promise I'll always be human if that's what you want."

She had a mental picture of lying on the floor near the fireplace, her body supported by a large polar bear as he napped underneath her as she read a book. Strangely, in her little flash fantasy, her tummy was large with their child. It was a sweet image that resonated with her, and she shook her head. "No, I don't mind hanging out with your bear sometimes, just not during intimacy. That's the only time I want to make sure you're all Kingston all the time."

Before dragging her closer for a kiss, he whispered, "Honey, I'm always Kingston all the time, bear or not, but I'll make sure my human Kingston is around when we're making love."

Satisfied with his promise, she cuddled closer and lifted her mouth to his. Her hand continued to stroke his shaft as the kiss deepened, while his hands went to her breasts. He stroked her nipples and thumbed them in slow circles that were tortuously delicious. She retaliated by dragging her hand slowly up and down his sensitive cock, pressing the palm against the underside to elicit a gasp from him. They were both soon worked up and ready, and she was thankful he was as naked as she was.

In seconds, she sat on him, guiding his cock inside her wet sheath, which took him in greedily, wanting all of his thickness. She clutched his shoulders, his arms wrapped tightly around her while they pressed against each other. She wanted all of him. Staring into his blue eyes, she was mesmerized by his perfect male beauty and the idea of spending the rest of her life with him.

She had the strangest urge and gave in to it, stretching forward and arching her neck so she could bite him on the shoulder.

He growled, sounding like a cross between a human and a bear, which she supposed was an accurate description, and his thrusts increased in intensity, as his cocked twitched inside her. A moment later, his teeth grazed her shoulder, biting deeper than she had. It caused a sharp start of pain, but only enhanced her pleasure, the final trigger for her orgasm. As her channel tightened around him, Kingston's erection hardened inside her and spasmed before he let loose a stream of warm release that spurted against her insides.

In the aftermath, she leaned against him, still holding him tightly. She didn't have to ask for clarification. The bite, while she didn't completely understand it, was clearly significant, and it had been the final step to making her his mate. He hadn't asked her if she was ready, but considering she had bitten him first, he'd clearly realized she had fully accepted everything he was offering.

It was crazy and bewildering to realize there was an entire group of people that she had never realized existed, the kind who could shift into animals at will. It would take some getting used to on an intellectual level, but emotionally and instinctively, she had already accepted the shift to a new reality.

She could accept anything, no matter how daunting or crazy, if it meant keeping Kingston in her life. He'd said bears recognized their mates, and she had the strangest sense she had also recognized hers, even as a human lacking his special senses.

6

A shley had been surprisingly difficult to find, and it
was going on two weeks with no sign of her. Grace
was trying to settle in to her new life as the mate
of a polar bear-shifter, while dealing with the upheaval of
moving from Calgary to Seattle, finding a new job, and
welcoming her friend back from her honeymoon.

Breanna had come back with a surprise that she had
whispered in confidence to Grace the day after they'd
returned. According to Rafe, she was expecting their first
baby, and though her body didn't know it yet, his bear
senses did.

Before learning about Ursus sapiens, she would have
feared for her friend's sanity, or at least her husband's sanity,
but now she believed him. How could she not, when she
knew Kingston had increased senses too?

Just because she wasn't focusing too much on Ashley
didn't mean Kingston had forgotten though, and she was
reminded of that again when her two bodyguards followed
her from the elevator into the waiting room where she was
interviewing for a records clerk position at the local hospi-

tal. She nodded to Jared and Sully before parting ways with them to sit near the door to wait to be called back for the interview.

She knew they didn't like waiting in the waiting room, but she couldn't explain their presence in the middle of an interview and still hope to keep a job. Or even acquire a job. Keeping it would be another matter, and she would have to decide how to handle security when she got a job.

She knew Kingston wouldn't like it, but she was probably going to insist on his staff waiting outside the building for her on a daily basis, rather than walking her in and babysitting her for hours at a time as she worked. It would be too unwelcome a distraction to both her and her coworkers to have bodyguards underfoot.

She knew his counterargument would include something along the lines of it would be an unwelcome distraction to have to face Ashley again in her panther-shifter form without security, but it seemed unlikely that the crazy woman would approach her in front of people.

In fact, it seemed unlikely Ashley would approach her at all, because it was taboo in shifter culture to seduce away another's mate, since most shifters mated for life. Ashley had already gotten herself into big trouble with their laws, and she didn't need to compound her error by continuing to pursue a married man. It would practically assure total banishment from shifter society, if she hadn't already guaranteed that with her murder attempt.

Her gaze darted to her left hand to stare at the large diamond gleaming up at her. They weren't officially married yet, but in his culture, they already were, having become so the minute he bit her. Still, she was looking forward to the human trappings of a wedding, and she knew her parents wouldn't want to miss that.

They were already slightly distraught that she was moving so far from home again, but she was going to try to persuade them to join her in her relocating. They were retired, and Kingston was receptive to the idea, so there was no reason they couldn't move with her, unless they chose not to. Everything was in place for her own happy ever-after, aside from the bothersome Ashley still being free.

A polished woman appeared at the doorway in a black pantsuit and red heels. "Grace DiPlaski?"

Grace stood up from the chair she had taken and walked over to meet her interviewer, extending her hand. "I'm Grace, and you must be Kelly?"

Kelly nodded, but didn't speak. She didn't react at all, other than to give a limp handshake.

A chill went down Grace's spine, especially when she saw the contempt in the other woman's eyes. She had been through this before, having submitted résumés and gone for interviews only to realize very quickly that the person conducting the interview had a fat bias, and they would never hire her in a million years, no matter how qualified she was. She really hoped that wasn't the case with Kelly, because the woman had contacted her based on her résumé posted on LinkedIn. Whatever the issue, clearly the woman didn't like something about her.

The other woman was tall, with long legs, and she made no concession for Grace's shorter legs. She hurried to catch up and keep up with her, her heels tapping on the linoleum floor. It was the industrial type that seemed common to all hospitals, but she was surprised to see it in the office area too. It was ugly, as was the rest of the utilitarian décor, but she didn't care as long as the job came with a decent salary and good benefits.

She didn't really have to worry about that, since

Kingston had a lot of money—the kind of money she couldn't even fathom—but she refused to let him pay her way for everything. She would stand on her own two feet and maintain a job, at least until they decided to have children someday soon. That was assuming she could find a job, which seemed unlikely, at least at this hospital based solely on Kelly's cold manner thus far.

They entered a small office/conference room. The other woman nodded briskly at her to take a seat, and then left the room, not speaking at all. The door was cracked open, so presumably she'd gone for something, but a word of explanation would have been nice.

Grace sat in the chair nearest the door, tapping her neatly trimmed nails on the mahogany table. This was the weirdest interview she'd ever been to, made doubly strange by the fact they had contacted her. She hadn't applied for this position at the hospital, because it hadn't been listed anywhere that she had seen during her job search. She'd never worked in medical records before, but Kelly had assured her that was fine when they'd spoken on the phone.

The other woman had been a lot warmer on the phone than in person, leading Grace back to the assumption that she had a problem with her curves. What did it matter, since she worked in back rooms mostly anyway? But it was better to know now than to take a job and end up working under a prejudiced bitch who would make her professional life miserable.

The door opening interrupted her reverie, and she plastered on a professional smile that melted from her face a second later, when she saw the identity of the new arrival. Ashley stood in the doorway, staring at her with a predatory look for a second before she closed the door with a click. The lock slid into place a moment later, and the white-haired woman made her way around the room to lower the blinds.

"What are you doing here?" demanded Grace, trying to keep any hint of fear out of her tone.

Ashley almost purred as she stretched across the table, not quite within reach, but close enough to be threatening. "I'm here to finish what I started. You're not good enough for him, and you won't take him from me." She raked Grace with a contemptuous look. "I can handle a bit of flirtation, though I don't know what he sees in you, but you're not going to steal my mate."

Grace rolled her eyes. "He's not your mate, and he never was. He never would have been and never will be. Even if you killed me, chopped me into bits, and scattered me in your kitty litter, he's never going to turn to you. Just let it go with some dignity, sweetie. You're turning into one of those psycho girls nobody wants to be around."

Ashley screeched at her, and halfway through the screech, it turned to a roar, as the other woman leapt at her, clothes ripping in the process as she shifted to her panther form.

Grace had been trying to keep Ashley distracted as she reached into her purse discreetly, fumbling for the items she had been carrying on her since Panther Lady had gone after her the first time. As Ashley reached her, barely raking her shoulder with razor-sharp claws, Grace let out a small cry of her own—one of pain mingled with triumph, as she lifted the pepper spray.

She had the perfect angle and didn't hesitate as she aimed the nozzle directly into Ashley's eyes, holding down the trigger until the other woman cried out with her cat cry again and flinched backward, pawing at her face.

Since Ashley could quickly recover, or at least enough to

be completely pissed off rather than severely impaired, Grace removed the second thing from her purse, a gift from Kingston. Sharp prongs extended when she pressed a button, and she touched them to the panther's side, turning it to full voltage to give the bitch the Tasering of a lifetime.

Ashley twitched and whimpered, squealing pathetically, but Grace didn't have pity on her. It wasn't until the other woman fell silent that she took away the Taser.

Slowly, she slid her chair backward, reaching into the purse for her cell phone to call her guards waiting outside. After speaking with Sully, she immediately called Kingston to tell him where she was.

He picked up as the men burst into the room, immediately going to Ashley's prone form. "Kelly?" he repeated after she had told him the details and was assured Sully and his partner were in the room with her. "As in Kelly Toth?"

"She said her name was Kelly Jones, but it could be Toth." Her eyes narrowed, and she glared at Ashley, who was starting to come around. As the woman's awareness returned, she shifted back to her human form, glaring at Grace. "Do you know Kelly Jones?"

Ashley sneered, though her voice was a weak imitation of what it had been a few moments before. "Kelly Toth," she said with a snarl.

"Her cousin," said Kingston in her ear, through the phone line. "Steer clear of that witch and Ashley until I get there. The trackers are also coming to pick her up, and Sully and Jared will do their best to clear out the department so there's little fuss or human involvement in the procurement of Ashley."

"Thank you for the Taser," she said to Kingston with a wicked grin, winking in Ashley's direction. She couldn't deny she enjoyed the gritted teeth and low growl coming from the other woman. "It was handy with this nasty little cat."

He laughed, though his voice still sounded concerned. "I'm glad you handled her, but are you okay?"

"I'm fine, love. It would take more than this white-haired witch to separate us."

"I'll be there soon as possible."

Grace nodded, though he couldn't see the motion on the phone. "I'll be waiting for you."

After hanging up, she slipped out of the conference room, no longer wanting to be in Ashley's proximity. Sully had remained with Ashley, and Jared accompanied her to the waiting room. It wouldn't take long to pick up her cousin, Jared assured her, but Grace wasn't overly concerned either way. She knew for certain Ashley would be dealt with, and it seemed likely Kelly would too. And just because Kelly had been willing to help her cousin orchestrate an opportunity to get to Grace didn't mean she was going to turn it into a crazy family vendetta and go after her.

She was surprisingly sanguine about the whole thing, still riding high on the tide of success, having dispatched Ashley by herself. If she could handle a psychotic panther-shifter out for her blood, she could handle anything.

Two men and a woman in black bodysuits arrived shortly thereafter, bearing a strange insignia she had never seen before on the patches adorning their biceps. They nodded to her and Sully before approaching, waiting for her guard to tell them where to find Ashley.

Ten minutes later, they came through with Ashley clapped in handcuffs and dressed in what looked like a janitor's coverall. Ashley glared at her as they moved past, digging in her heels to say one last thing. "If he'd rather have you, he's not worthy of me. You two deserve each other."

"Yes, we certainly do," said Grace with a large grin. "Now run along and stop being a bad kitty."

The other woman's eyes flashed with fire, but she stopped digging in her heels as the trackers nudged her forward. In seconds, the white-haired woman was gone, and Grace was confident she would never see her again.

Kingston arrived a few moments later, and he swept her into his arms for several kisses and a long embrace before he seemed assured she was okay. When he pulled back, his expression was one of regret. "I'm sorry this happened. I thought we had a plan, and it's my job to protect you."

She cupped his face, pressing her palm against his cheek. "Honey, you did protect me. You're the one who gave me the Taser. We knew she might pop up again. You can't blame yourself for this. I was prepared, and nothing bad happened."

"But it could have. I would've lost you, and if you're gone, what's the point of anything? My happiness is all tied up with yours."

Her heart melted at his words, and she softened her voice further while she stretched forward to press a gentle kiss to the side of his lips. "We'll just have to make sure we keep each other happy then, my love." She kissed the other side of his lips. "We have the rest of our lives to get that right."

"We don't need any help or practice at that. You make me happy just being here." He kissed her full on the mouth, his passion clearly rising.

Hers was mounting too, and she vaguely entertained the idea of finding the janitor's closet, assuming there must be one since Ashley had worn a janitor's coveralls after her arrest. "I love you, Kingston."

He growled, that pleasing growl of possession that made her shiver with delight. "I love you too."

Hand-in-hand, they walked from the hospital in search of an expedient place to mate that didn't involve a janitor's closet. She was looking forward to a lifetime of this—of little moments of quiet happiness interspersed with the bigger explosions of joyous events. She would be content to be by his side for the rest of her life, whether they were curled up by the fire reading a book or planning their wedding. There would be countless moments like those, since they were mating for life.

BONUS EXCERPT: THE BEAR'S SECRET BABY

Shayla shivered faintly as the first sight of the island appeared in the mist the closer the boat drew to it. It looked ominous, though she supposed that was more to do with her own perception based on what Lila had told her, and the boat captain's reaction when she'd asked him to give them a ride to the island. He'd seemed to regard her as crazy and had tried to talk her out of coming there.

The gruff old man came up behind her, as though her thoughts had summoned him. "That's Bear Island," he said in a rough tone.

She nodded. "Yes, I thought it must be, since we're heading right for it." The island was unofficially named Bear Island, according to the captain, though it had no official name. Existing as part of the San Juan Islands chain in the Strait of Juan de Fuca, it was officially uninhabited. Apparently, Kade Lassiter and his people felt otherwise, because they had inhabited it for several generations, at least according to her sister Lila.

"Are you sure about staying, Miss Dalton?" The captain scratched his white beard and sent her a look of disapproval. "Like I said, I won't be back for another month with a delivery of supplies. I can't promise you'll be able to get off the island until then, and the people who live there aren't exactly warm and friendly."

Shayla squared her shoulders and ran a hand down the bundle in the sling. "I'm sure." She wasn't actually sure. She was terrified at the prospect, but she had run out of ideas, and no one else had had the answers as to why her baby niece was not growing despite a healthy start in life.

With a sigh, the captain moved away from her, and they docked at the island less than fifteen minutes later. As the boat's crew, which consisted of three men including the captain, started to unload the supplies, three other inhabitants appeared, seeming to solidify from the mist itself, and their eyes were wide with shock when they saw her step off the boat.

She ignored their response, hesitating for a moment before approaching the youngest-looking one. He might have been in his early twenties. His expression wasn't quite as hard and unwelcoming as the other two flanking him. She forced a small smile, because she couldn't make it any larger with a sudden bout of nerves seizing her, and looked up at him. "Could you please tell me where I could find Kade Lassiter?"

"Who wants to know?" asked one of the men standing behind the younger one, his expression stern, and his voice unfriendly.

"That's personal. If you could just tell me where to find him, I'll get out of your way."

"Outsiders aren't welcome here," said the one who hadn't spoken yet, his unfriendly expression matching the man beside him.

She turned a pleading gaze to the younger man, pinning all her hopes on him. "Please. It's really important."

After a moment, the younger man lifted a hand and waved it vaguely in the direction from which he and the other two had come. "Keep walking straight down the road, until you come to the sheriff's office. That's where you'll find Kade."

She nodded her thanks and hurried away before the other two with him could intercept her, or try to force her back onto the boat. As she hurried through the small village, she was careful to avoid making eye contact with anyone she came across. There weren't many people out on the main street, but she still felt like eyes were on her the entire time as she traversed the length of the town. She shivered as she remembered the conversation she'd had with Lila three days ago.

"You don't want to go to that island for any reason."

Shayla had protested, "It's for Aislinn. Something has to happen. I have to do something, and maybe her father's family knows something we don't. Genetics or something..."

Lila had laughed bitterly. "Genetics. Yeah, that's it. Just stay away from that whole cult."

Shayla had probed before, but her sister had always refused to expound on what she meant by cult when she referred to Kade and his people. At the time, she had issued a small sigh. "Lila, she's your daughter. You can't want her to die."

Lila had sounded cold and utterly convincing when she'd said, "I don't care either way. I would've gotten rid of it if I could have."

Shayla had felt the familiar surge of irritation and bewilderment at her sister's lack of maternal feelings for her daughter, but she had tamped them down. "Fine, if you don't care about Aislinn, then tell me how to get to the island so that I can help her, and do it for me. You still love me, don't you?"

Lila's tone had softened marginally. "Of course I do, even though I don't understand your need to keep that thing. We could have just given it to the foster system, and someone else could have adopted it."

Shayla had persisted, until Lila had finally told her how to find Bear Island.

Now, recalling her sister's words, she wasn't certain if she was allowing them to taint her impression of the town, or if it was simply her own observations and the general air of unwelcome that clung to the place. Whatever it was, she felt like an outsider and vulnerable to attack. It was a ridiculous notion, because people didn't just attack someone for entering their town, but instinct warned her to turn around and run back to the boat.

She might have listened to the fear guiding her if it hadn't been for Aislinn curled against her chest in a warm little bundle. The baby hadn't roused much during the boat ride, or before that. She was so listless and nearly lifeless that it broke Shayla's heart and hardened her resolve to stay. She was probably pinning her hopes on something that wouldn't help either, but she wasn't leaving until she spoke to the child's father and ruled out all possibilities of helping Aislinn.

With her determination renewed, she crossed the last few feet to the sheriff's office before opening the door. As she stepped through the doorway, she took a deep breath for courage and slipped inside the small office.

Small was right. It consisted of one room, with a single jail cell in the corner, currently unoccupied. She was afraid she'd found the sheriff not in, but there was a man seated at the desk in the corner, and he looked up at her as the door closed behind her.

For a moment, she forgot why she was there. His sheer

male perfection stole her breath, and her eyes greedily gobbled up the sight for a moment as she appreciated the wide set of his shoulders, the perfect angles of his face, and the rich brown hair that invited her fingers to run through it. Or might have, if his expression hadn't been so stony. The visible reminder of how unwelcome she was jerked her out of her feminine reverie, and she straightened her shoulders as she walked closer to the desk, not waiting for an invitation.

"Who are you?" he asked gruffly, but his voice was smooth as dark chocolate, with a touch of whiskey.

"My name is Shayla Dalton—"

His nostrils flared, and his unwelcome expression grew darker. "Dalton? As in Lila Dalton?"

She nodded, bracing herself.

"Get out."

Shayla shook her head and planted her feet firmly on the floor as she stood in front of his desk, temporarily eschewing the chair in front of it. "No. I can't do that."

He scowled at her. "If you're here because of Lila, you can just turn around and walk right out again. I haven't seen her in months, and I want nothing more to do with her."

She shrugged. "Lucky for you, Lila feels the same way. I'm not here about Lila though."

His scowl deepened as he leaned back in his chair, crossing his arms over his chest. "What brings you to our island then, Shayla Dalton?"

With a deep breath, Shayla slipped off her jacket, which had been a necessity for the early morning boat ride, even though it was early summer. She laid it on the chair in front of the desk before folding down the corner of the sling so he could see the baby's face. "Your daughter brings me here, Kade Lassiter."

***

Kade was temporarily frozen in shock at the woman's words. He wanted to reject them, but he found himself rising from his desk chair instead and moving around the furniture to get closer to the woman and the baby. "Let me hold her."

The Dalton woman hesitated, clearly torn for a moment before she slipped the baby from the sling carefully, handing over the tiny bundle.

Kade could hold her in one hand, though he used a second one to support her. She was tiny and nearly lifeless, and a dart of concern shot through him. He brought her closer to his face, inhaling her scent from the crown of her head, and his bear rumbled inside him. She was theirs. She smelled like them. This baby was his daughter, and Lila hadn't ever bothered to tell him she was pregnant. His bear roared, and it took all of Kade's control to keep from surrendering to the urge to growl at the other woman standing before him, to direct his sudden rage for Lila toward her instead. "You've brought the baby. Now get off the island before the boat leaves."

Her mouth dropped open, and her green eyes sparkled with dismay that turned to anger. "I'm not a delivery person dropping off your child. I'm in the process of adopting Aislinn, and I'm not going anywhere without her."

"She's mine, and I'll take care of her. You can go now."

The woman, who seemed small to him, though she was above-average height for a human woman, looked like she wanted to stomp her foot at him. She was clearly enraged, and though it should have provoked his temper, it simply brought a surge of amusement instead. He was quick to smother it, along with ignoring his bear's interest in the woman before him. After Lila, he had no intention of getting involved with a woman again.

"I'm not leaving my niece. She's sick, and I'm hoping your people can help her. Lila said you were into...strange things." She looked discomfited as she said the words. "I'm not judging anything. I just hope you can help. The doctors at the Children's Hospital in San Francisco have run out of ideas."

He looked down again at his daughter, already feeling a strong bond forming with her. A surge of anger and dismay shot through him at the idea of the little one not making it. "What's wrong with her?" For one thing, he could guess she wasn't growing properly. She was tiny, and though she couldn't be very old, she should have been larger than she was, especially with her shifter heritage.

"I'm not sure. She was born early, but really healthy. Aislinn weighed almost nine pounds, and she was alert, with good Apgar scores. For the first three or four days, everything was fine, though she lost weight, which is expected. The problem became obvious when she didn't start regaining the weight. At first, she just maintained, but recently, she started to lose ounces that she can't afford to lose. Her main pediatrician has diagnosed her with failure to thrive, and they did a genetic panel to determine if she has a genetic disorder, but everything came back normal."

Kade stiffened slightly at that news, surprised everything had come back normal. There should have been markers or something about her DNA that alerted officials his daughter wasn't quite human. He was relieved they hadn't been able to detect her *ursa sapien* genes, but it was strange. "What have they done for her?"

The Dalton woman reeled off several things, her discouragement obvious as she reached the end of the list.

"Nothing's working. Even the high-calorie formula isn't doing the trick."

Kade nodded, having an inkling of what was wrong, but uncertain. "I want to take her to see my grandmother. Tula raised me, my father, and my six uncles. She might know what to do." He wasn't asking permission, and she seemed to realize that.

She nodded. "We're ready."

He pushed back a surge of irritation, realizing he was stuck with her, at least temporarily. He still had every intention of sending her on her way and keeping Aislinn, but now wasn't the time to argue about that. First, they had to focus on the baby.

ABOUT THE AUTHOR

Paranormal romance author Aria Chase combines her fascination with the occult and her undying love for happily ever after to create steamy shifter reads that are perfect for devouring in one night.

Connect with Aria online:

www.ariachase.com

ALSO BY ARIA CHASE

Emerald City Shifters

Bearly Breathing

The Bear's Secret Baby

One Night With A Bear

Fighting For Her Bear

Bought By A Bear

Sundown Wolves

Temptation

Reparation

Distraction